Little Nemo's Journey to Slumberland

Nemo's Slumberland Adventures
Book 1

Nathaniel Matthews

For Philip

&

A special thank you to Winsor McCay
His dream endures.

Nemo's Slumberland Adventures

Little Nemo's Journey to Slumberland

Little Nemo's Journey to Slumberland
THE GOLDEN GATE

Little Nemo's Journey to Slumberland
THE GOLDEN PALACE

Little Nemo's Escape from Slumberland

Coming Soon:

Little Nemo's Escape from Slumberland
INTO THE DARKNESS

Little Nemo's Escape from Slumberland
A BRIDGE TO THE STARS

Dare to dream

It can be hard to explain Slumberland, mostly because it is constantly shifting and changing. What can be said is that it is a magical place, woven from the fabric of dreams. It is a place of rainbows and unicorns, dragons and castles, flying horses and endless oceans. Sometimes, there are places that the sun never sets; other times there are places of infinite darkness. It is likely to find a trail that never ends, and just as likely to find one that goes to the edge of the world. It is so vast, that all of the people in the world can visit and not be in the same place, never see each other, and spend their whole lives coming and going, never seeing the same thing twice. The world we live in is just a speck in Slumberland. In fact, there are many, many copies of our world in Slumberland, although rarely are they exact copies.

There is one place, however, that does not shift and change like all the rest. There is one place that we are not permitted to visit. In the very center of Slumberland is a city with high golden walls and in the center of the city is the Golden Palace. All of the shifting and changing, and all the spots we visit, are on the outside of the walls and far away. If a visitor to Slumberland pays attention, they may

The Golden Palace shimmers in the distance.

see the palace shimmering on the horizon, although few ever take notice. Our story begins in the Golden Palace.

****

King Morpheus had the look of a great Roman God. He wore a crown of golden leaves that sat upon his bald head. He had tufts of white hair around his ears that ran into his long, full beard that covered his lower face completely. The beard was snow white and so long it reached nearly to his belly button. He wore a white toga with a golden clasp, and thick golden arm bands around his biceps. He had a long nose that came to a point, one that was long from brow to tip but did not protrude far from his face. It brought to mind a great bird of prey, perhaps a bald eagle. His eyes were piercing blue, with deep wrinkles at the sides from years of full hearted

King Morpheus

laughs and smiles. His eyebrows were gray and bushy. He was well aged in appearance, but also strong, and heavily muscled.

He sat on his throne, tapping his fingers and clenching his jaw. He had a tendency to tap his fingers when he was nervous or worried. The princess was ill. She had stopped eating, and now spent most of her time locked in her room. King Morpheus knew exactly what she needed. Like him, she was part star, and needed a companion to keep her spirit grounded. The companion had to be an earth boy, so she could be tethered to him for life. If an earth boy was not found, she would have to take to the heavens and become a fixed point of light, or stay in the Slumberland palace and fade away.

Morpheus knew all of this, because he went through it when he

A former Slumberland queen takes her place in the stars.

was her age, just as every King and Queen of Slumberland before him. He had ruled for a thousand years, and although Slumberland greatly extended the life of mortals who stayed, he always knew the time would come when his beloved wife would age and pass on to the next world. The princess was his only heir, the future Queen, and with the passing of her mother, a woman of the real world whom Morpheus had been tethered to since they were children, King Morpheus himself had limited time before he would have to take his place in the night sky.

He had to ensure his daughter's future, not only because he loved her, but for the good of Slumberland as well. Without a King or Queen the palace would collapse, and what order they maintained would be lost. Without a constant balance between

Slumberland and the real world, both worlds would die. Slumberland existed through the dreams of all men and women, but also was its own place, with its own thriving magical beings living within it, and the magic of Slumberland fed the creative minds of the dreamers. Without Slumberland, people's creative spirits would be suppressed, and they would not find restoration in sleep. Without a King or Queen, at first the world would fall into a tired state that lacked the ability to invent and create great works of art. Eventually, the sleeping and awake worlds would fall into chaos and then collapse in on themselves.

So, Morpheus sat tapping his fingers, waiting for the star imps. They were late, but that was not much of a surprise, because they barely grasped the concept of time. When finally they arrived, they came down the walkway of the throne room tripping over each other and giggling. There were seven of them in total. They had the appearance of wearing a one piece body suit, all black and covered in stars. They had white boots and white gloves, and thick white pleated ruffled collars. They were bald, with bleach white skin, and a small tuff of red hair on top of their heads. They all looked exactly the same, with long faces, long pointy chins, and big mouths often smiling a large toothy grin. King Morpheus had asked for all of the star imps to be present. He knew that they would not understand that concept, but had hoped for more than seven. Star imps existed only at night, when the sky was clear, being that they only existed as a materialized form of the light of the stars. When the light reached earth, it was reflected through the prism of reality and changed by the time it reached Slumberland. The star imps were a manifestation of that reflection, and so there was the potential for there to be as many imps as stars visible in the night sky. They were highly respected, because they were fractional reflections of past kings and queens, but as a fraction, their personalities were not always quite whole. Also, as star light, they mixed to a point that they lost themselves, and so they often talked of themselves as if they were all the same person, the many being one and one being the many, so there was no telling how many would actually show up.

"King Morpheus," started one as he bowed.

"His Royal Majesty," another added, moving shoulder to shoulder with the one who spoke previously and also bowing.

The other five then fell into line, bowing and saying together, "How may I be of service?" (Except one, who said "we" instead of "I")

"Each of you shines on the real world before arriving here, correct?" asked King Morpheus.

"Yes, your grace," said one in the middle.

"Not exactly," started the one next to him.

"Not exactly," said the one who had bowed first, "we actually shine on the real world even now."

"Even now," the one on the opposite end continued, "we shine on the real world. If we are here…"

"We are there too," the one in the middle finished.

King Morpheus nodded, "very good, very good, and so I do require your assistance," he said.

"Anything for you," said one just right of the middle.

"We will do anything," said the one in the middle.

"We will do what we can," said the one just left of the middle.

"I need you to find me a boy. One who will have the ability to come here in his real form and stay."

"How will we know him, your grace," they all said together.

"Your light will pass through him a little, I think, as he sleeps, because the real him is not fully in the real world."

"We will look," said one.

"We will try our best," said another.

"I have found him," said the ones on each end at the same time.

"He is Nemo," the one in the middle said, all the others nodded.

"Wonderful. Nemo, yes. You are

excused, my noble starlights. I am very thankful for your help," the King exclaimed with a beaming smile. The star imps bowed once more in unison, and exited the throne room. As they left the King realized there was now eight of them, and wondered when the other appeared.

He then exited the throne room himself and went to the courtyard in the center of the palace. He expected he would find Oomp there.

****

Oomp was one of King Morpheus's most trusted councils. He had been counseling the King for many years, and seemed to have a deep connection and understanding of other's emotions. He had come to Slumberland as the imaginary friend of a boy from the real world, and in Slumberland found a permanent existence. The boy had long since passed to the next world, and Oomp still carried a deep sense of sorrow over losing his creator. He was not an unhappy fellow by any means, but his sense of loss and sorrow made him more real, and gave him more understanding of the real world. This all added to his value as a king's council.

"Oomp, are you here," King Morpheus called as he entered the courtyard.

Oomp popped out from behind a pillar; he was trimming vines that wrapped around it. Maintaining the shrubs, bushes and vines of the courtyards was one of his favorite hobbies. "Here your Majesty," he called, hurrying towards the King.

Oomp looked like the ringmaster of a circus, which was not surprising considering the boy who imagined him did so shortly after attending the circus. He wore a long dove tailed jacket with a red color and cuffs, and large golden buttons. Under the jacket was a white poet blouse. His pants were black and tucked into his white boots. On his head was a tall top hat, black with long red triangles that ran from the rim halfway up to the top. His face was pale and smooth, with a gentle look to it that a child would find comforting.

"Oomp, his majesty requests the presence of Little Nemo. The star imps know where to find him. I am trusting you to make sure he arrives, as soon as possible. The princess cannot wait much longer."

"I will see to it myself, my King."

****

In the real world, in a real city, on a real street, the sun was setting, dipping below the rooftops of the real houses. Inside one of those real houses, a real family with a real seven-year-old boy were eating dinner at a real dining room table. The boy seemed normal enough, but looks could be deceiving. He was actually quite extraordinary, and we now meet him, right before his great adventures begin.

Nemo finished his dinner and looked at his empty plate dissatisfied. "I'm still hungry," he said to his parents.

"There's no more dinner to eat," replied his mother.

Nemo kept his big brown eyes down, continuing to look at his empty plate. "Isn't there something else?"

"I could take a bit more too," said his father, "how about some Welsh rarebit, I can warm it up, I'm certain we have some from breakfast. What do you say Nemo?"

Nemo looked up from his plate

with a smile, nodding his head.

"I do think he has had enough, dear," Mother interjected, "eating too much will give him nightmares. Especially something as rich as that."

"Just a slice, I'm sure he will be fine, won't you sport?"

"Yeah, Mom, I'll be okay, and I'm really hungry."

"Okay," his mom gave in, "just don't be calling for me when you wake up tonight."

****

After dinner Nemo squeezed in a bit of playtime, as any boy of seven would do when the opportunity presented itself. Then, at his parent's insistence, he got himself ready for bed. He bathed, put on his pajamas, and somewhat tamed his mop of dark brown hair so that it wasn't too difficult in the morning. He brushed his teeth, two less than a week before, because the front ones on top had come out and his adult teeth had yet to come in. He then made his way to his room and climbed in bed.

"Mom, Dad, I'm ready," he called out.

His parents came into his room, smiling. His dad gave him his last drink of water, as he did every night, and his mother tucked him in, as she did every night. There were hugs and kisses on the cheeks, and then his parents left with a "good night" and "I love you."

Nemo lay with his eyes open for a few minutes, looking up at the glowing star stickers that covered his bedroom ceiling. He felt the exhaustion of the day start to take him over, and his eyelids grew heavy. Each blink became longer until finally, his eyes stayed closed, and Nemo drifted into a deep, comfortable sleep.

"Excuse me, young sir."

Nemo stirred a little, pulling the covers up closer to his chin, and rolled on his side. Did he just hear something? No, certainly not. He kept his eyes closed, and continued to sleep.

A clearing of a throat, "Ehh-Em," and still Nemo lay motionless with his eyes closed.

"Excuse me, Master Nemo; I must insist you give me your attention."

This time Nemo couldn't ignore the talking. He rolled to his back and opened his eyes, looking around his dark room. He sat up, and realized that there was a very curious figure standing at the end of his bed, but it was hard to focus on, and maybe, just maybe, not there at all. He rubbed his eyes, and when he looked again he saw it rather clearly. It looked to be the ringmaster from a circus, although, not quite that maybe.

"Hello Master Nemo, please do not be frightened. I am Oomp, from the Golden Palace of Slumberland. You are requested to appear before His Majesty, King Morpheus of Slumberland. I have been sent to retrieve you, should you be willing to come."

"Slumberland?" Nemo asked, still processing what was happening.

"Yes, the place of dreams, a magical world of imagination and ideas. His Majesty Morpheus is King, and has extended an invitation for you to appear at the Golden Palace, a very rare honor for a boy of this world."

Nemo was not fully sure of what was going on, but he was delighted and honored to have his presence requested by a king. He also figured that it was not a good thing to deny a kings request.

"Okay. But, I do wonder, how did

you get here, and how do I get there?"

"No worries, Master Nemo. I will help you. How I got here is simple, and how we get there, though a bit more complicated, is not important, because it is not always the same. Much of how we get there depends on you, because you are the one who can change it. The problem is if you don't know how to change it, you won't be able to. One thing you can't change is that it is a long way off through many miles of weird scenes."

"I don't understand," said Nemo honestly.

"No worries, my boy. If you believe that we can make it there, everything else will fall in line. Can you think of a good way for us to go a long way?"

"Well, I guess a horse can take a person where they need to go."

"Very good, Master Nemo, and so a horse it is! I happen to have one here," Oomp said excitedly as he stepped aside and motioned to the corner of the room behind him.

"But… I don't see a… yes maybe…"

"Just rub that sleep from your eyes and look. His name is Somnus; he is a spotted night horse. A wonderful creature! Surely you see him now?"

And Nemo did, there, as if appearing out of nowhere was the magnificent beast, stomping its hoof and shaking its mane. It was not as big as the horses Nemo had seen pulling carriages in the city. This one was actually much smaller, but the perfect size for him. Somnus was white, with large irregular black spots. His tale was white with a thick black ring in the middle, and his mane was all white and shining even in the scarce moonlight coming through Nemo's window. On his forehead, directly between his eyes, was a red jewel that

Nemo meets Oomp and Somnus.

looked as if it were part of him, not just a decoration.

Nemo climbed out of bed and approached the horse, reaching up and stroking his nose gently.

"He's beautiful," he said in awe.

"Yes, and gentle as can be. Tonight the way to Slumberland is in the sky and through the clouds. Somnus can take you there. Just be warned that the farther you go, the more you distance yourself from the real world, then the stranger things may be. Keep steady. Don't run Somnus too hard, though he has no limits, you still may."

Nemo nodded, though he may not have been fully listening, being so distracted by the wonder of Somnus. He put his foot in the stirrup and leapt onto Somnus's back without a problem. It felt comfortable and natural on the horses back. Nemo leaned forward and stroked the horse's neck. Somnus leaned into Nemo's hand out of appreciation for the affection.

"Now, ride Nemo. Somnus knows the way. To the sky and through the clouds. I'll see you on the other side, in Slumberland," said Oomp, and as he talked he opened Nemo's window, and as he opened it, it grew much larger than it was before, large enough for Somnus and Nemo to fit through with room to spare. Somnus turned towards the opening, leaping out into the night sky. Nemo turned back to thank Oomp, but he was already gone, the window closed and back to its normal size.

****

Somnus moved his legs as if he was running on the ground like a normal horse, but he was not a normal horse, and he and Nemo were not on the ground. Somnus galloped through the air, and they climbed ever up, closer and closer to the clouds. He was moving quickly, but Nemo noted that the ride was perfectly smooth, and he was sure he could go much faster. He clicked his heels against Somnus and leaned close to one of his ears, telling him so, "faster, Somnus, faster." Somnus obeyed, the wind rippled Nemo's pajamas, and the clouds drew ever nearer.

Soon they were amongst the clouds, and Somnus leveled out, no longer climbing higher. He instead rode forward through the heavy mist and fog of the clouds. For Nemo, the sense of flying was almost lost, as it could have well been a ride on a very foggy morning. Somnus kept pushing forward, and Nemo noted to himself that even at this speed the ride was rather smooth. He was sure that he could handle Somnus going a bit faster. Again he clicked his heels against Somnus and leaned closer to one of his ears, "faster, Somnus, faster," and Somnus obeyed.

Somnus was moving at an incredible speed. Nemo couldn't help but think things were changing, somehow, as they ripped through the clouds. Faintly, it seemed, he could hear the striking of hooves against the ground. He leaned the best he could and looked down, wondering if they had actually come down out of the clouds into a dense fog, and if they were back on land. He could see nothing but white. From the corner of his eye he thought he saw another form in the clouds. He looked and strained to see, but couldn't decide if there was something there or not. Then he heard a noise off to the other side, and turning that direction thought he might see something there as well, a shadow through the fog and mist maybe. He couldn't help but feel a little scared not being able to see what flanked him on each side, and so decided that it would be best for Somnus to just outrun whatever it was. He clicked his heels against Somnus, but this time didn't have to tell him to go faster. As soon as Somnus felt the heel clicks he quickened his pace.

The sound of hooves striking the ground grew louder, and now Nemo was sure that he could see ground below them, although it didn't seem fully solid, as if it were still halfway sky. The fog began to thin, and Nemo was surprised to see that the two figures on each side of him and Somnus were still there, and keeping pace. They were becoming more and more visible, and the closest figure did not gallop like Somnus, but seemed rather to hop and bound. At first Nemo thought it was a giant rabbit maybe, but as they went further and further, and the fog cleared more and more, he began to see the figures around him more clearly. He realized the closest was actually a kangaroo, and it had a rider.

There were other animals too, a large cat, and a pig were close by. They all had riders, but the riders were not people. The furthest from him was the pig, and on its back was a gray rabbit. The cat came up on his right side, and looked to be carrying a bright orange frog. The one on the kangaroo was a ring tailed lemur; it caught up to him on his left side. The lemur on the kangaroo and the frog on the cat began to veer in closer to Nemo and Somnus. Nemo clicked his heals against Somnus again, and the night horse again went faster, but the

Nemo rides Somnus on his way to Slumberland.

others kept up still.

"Ahoy!" yelled the lemur.

"Hello, friend!" yelled the frog.

Having them yell greetings and call him friend made Nemo relax. Seeing them more clearly now, they looked innocent enough, and were actually smiling, seemingly enjoying the fast paced ride. They were going so fast now that Nemo had to hold on tightly, feeling that he would fly off the night horse's back if he relaxed too much.

"Hello," Nemo called out, "you scared me a little, before I could see you clearly."

"Oh, dear! Very sorry about that," shouted the frog.

"Very sorry, indeed. I don't think anyone has thought I was scary before. We just love to ride fast, and you are riding very fast," exclaimed the lemur.

"Very fast indeed," agreed the

frog.

"Yes, Somnus is a very good horse," Nemo replied.

As they shouted back in forth to each other, needing to yell because at the speed they traveled the wind causes quite a ruckus; the fog that enshrouded them all but fell away. They were surrounded by the clear night sky, with the stars and moon shining like Nemo had never seen before. Nemo could hear the pounding of Somnus's hooves clearly now, as well as the thumps of the kangaroo when it landed in between bounds. Looking down, though, caused Nemo's head to swim a little, as the ground seemed to shimmer and still sometimes seemed to not be there at all. The Lemur noticed Nemo looking down.

"Slumberland is what you're seeing. Just not quite there yet," explained the lemur.

"Oh. How strange," said Nemo. He hoped it wouldn't be too much further. Holding on to Somnus was getting harder and harder.

"I have an idea. Being so close now, how's about a race?" suggested the frog.

"What a wonderful idea," replied the lemur, "although, I don't think Nemo could keep up."

"Yes I could," Nemo exclaimed, insulted.

"I don't know. We can go much faster," said the frog.

"So can I, let's have at it then," shouted Nemo, and he began knocking his heels against the night horse over and over.

In no time, Somnus distanced himself from the other animals, and he just kept going faster and faster. Nemo felt himself sliding back on the saddle, bouncing with each stride so hard that his hands began to slip. This was too much for him, and he felt foolish for accepting the challenge. He was only seven, after all, and the dream was becoming overwhelming, it was becoming much too frightening. He started to cry, wanting it all to end.

"Momma... Momma, come help me. Mom," he sobbed.

Far away, he cried. Far away, his mom heard.

A giant golden eagle flew up next to him, with all its might trying to keep up with the night horse. Oomp was seated on the eagles back.

"Nemo, I warned you not to push too hard. Grab my hand, you can do it," shouted Oomp.

"No, I can't. Momma, help me..."

Nemo's mom was up now, putting on her robe.

Oomp reached as far as he could,

but Nemo was too scared to release the reigns of Somnus. The horse continued to accelerate, and soon Oomp and the eagle were far behind. Nemo could hold on no longer, and he flew from the night horse's back. The ground was not solid enough to support a real boy, and Nemo fell through it into darkness. He fell and fell, away from the shimmering image of Slumberland, away from Somnus, away from the stars and the moon, he fell into complete darkness, crying and calling for his mother, until suddenly...

Nemo landed, bounced, twisted, and with a thud found himself half wrapped in his blanket on the floor next to his bed, one leg still perched up on the mattress. He was still crying. His bedroom door opened and he could see the outline of his mother in the doorway.

"Oh, Nemo, what did I tell you at

Nemo dreams of falling after losing control of Somnus.

Nemo tumbles out of bed as he wakes up.

dinner. I should go wake your father. He's part to blame, after all. This is the last time you get Welsh rarebit that late."

She untangled his blankets and helped him back into bed. She rubbed his back until he calmed down.

****

Oomp walked down the long hallway to the King's reading chamber slowly, still working out how he would explain his failure. King Morpheus was a gentle and merciful man, slow to anger so it wasn't punishment that worried Oomp. Oomp so loved the king and his daughter, the princess, that he was anguished to disappoint them. He reached the large, wooden double doors and stopped, took a deep breath, removed his top hat and walked in.

"Excuse my interruption, Your Majesty," said Oomp as the king looked up from a rather large book named "The Dreaming Habits of Adolescence" and smiled.

"No, of course Oomp, this is no bother. I have been waiting on your return rather impatiently," replied the king as he stood, towering over Oomp, and moved towards him with a clap of his hands in excitement. "So, where is the boy? Where is little Nemo?"

Oomp fiddled with the rim of his top hat and could not meet the king's eyes. He began to cry, softly.

"Oomp, my dear friend, tell me what happened," King Morpheus said gently, his almost ever present smile disappearing and replaced with a look of concern. He put a hand on Oomp's back and led him to a long plush couch, having him take a seat and then sitting down next to him.

"I am so sorry, My King. I have failed. I thought a night horse would be a good way to get him here quickly, but it was too much for such a young boy, and he fell back to the real world."

"Hmm... I see. It is a difficult journey to the palace for any boy to make. Never has it fell to one so young, though. There's time enough to try again tonight. Don't despair, Oomp. We must try again. I need you to come up with a better plan."

"I could use some help, perhaps, your Grace? Maybe the star imps could be of some service?"

King Morpheus asked Oomp what he had in mind, and Oomp explained his plan. The king agreed and summoned the star imps to see if they could do what Oomp had proposed.

****

"So, is it possible?" asked King Morpheus. Five star imps stood in front of him.

"Very tricky, but…" started the one farthest to the left.

"We could try," said the one standing next to him.

"I could certainly try," said the one in the middle.

"I would be stretched very thin…" said the one farthest to the right.

"We would be there, and here, and there again," said the one next to him.

"I need you to try," ordered King Morpheus, "for the sake of your princess. Meet Oomp in the courtyard and leave at once. There is no time to waste."

The Star Imps bowed together and hurried to Oomp. He was waiting for them just as the king had said. Together, they traveled back to Nemo's bedroom to try once more to lead him to the Golden Palace at the center of Slumberland.

****

Nemo's mother left, and he soon began to fall back to sleep. As he drifted away, he heard some strange noises, and felt his bed being lifted and shook. He sat up to have a look, and was surprised and perplexed by what he saw. Oomp was there again, and seemed to be directing a strange looking group in the customization of his bed. Even stranger, as he watched, his room dissolved around him, and he was not in his room anymore, but in the middle of the street outside his house.

"Good night, Master Nemo. I wondered when you would notice us. I must apologize for the way our last meeting ended, rather unfortunate, and just as we were getting close. We are nearly ready to depart. This time, I'm sure, will go much, much better," said Oomp.

"Oomp, who are they?" Nemo

The star imps transform Nemo's bed into a chariot.

asked of the five Star Imps. Four of them were lifting his bed, and the fifth was attaching what looked like wheels made of large golden disks to each corner.

"They are star imps, Nemo, but there will be time for explanations and introductions later."

The star imps finished with the wheels and moved to the front of his bed, Nemo kicked his blankets off and moved closer to see what they were doing. They attached a golden plate to the wood by touching spots with their fingers, and after a flash of sparks and light, it seemed to be secured to their satisfaction. After the plate was secure, they attached four large golden rings to it in the same manner. To each of the four golden rings they tied a silver rope, and the silver ropes were set up to drive two very large night horses that the star imps were working to connect to the bed-chariot. If not for the size, he could have sworn one of them was Somnus. He thought it funny that he had not noticed them before.

The star imps seemed to be making some last minute adjustments. Two went to the rear wheel of the bed and kneel down, and after some work, Nemo wasn't really sure what they did, only one stood up. Nemo moved to that side of the bed to see what the other was doing, but it seemed to have vanished.

"You there," Nemo said to the one, "where did the other star imp go?"

"There was no other," it replied, "only me."

Nemo leaned over the side of his bed and looked beneath. There was nothing to see. When he sat back up, he looked around and could only count two star imps now, both tending to the horses. They came towards Nemo, one on each side of his bed.

"Ready to go?" asked the one to Nemo's left.

"Yes, I think so," replied Nemo as he looked towards the star imp that was speaking. He then turned back to the one on his right side, but he was now gone. "Where did all your friends go, the other star imps?" Nemo asked.

"Friends?" The star imp questioned, looking a bit confused. "I assure you, I am the only star imp there is."

"Oh. I'm sorry; I just find things from Slumberland can be confusing. You are from Slumberland too, right?"

"I am from here and there," answered the star imp.

"I see," Nemo replied, although he actually was very confused, "well, my name is Nemo. What's yours?"

"Nice to meet you, Nemo, my name is Star. Star Imp."

Nemo laughed a little and said, "Well, I guess I kinda already knew that."

The star imp picked up the reigns, and with a flick of his wrists they were off. They sat against the headboard of the bed, and the night horses accelerated so fast that Nemo felt himself being pushed back against it. The star imp continued to flick the reigns, and every time he did Nemo felt a jolt as they added more speed. Everything was a blur. They passed house after house, building after building, so fast that they all ran together. The street lamps became streams of light, and soon they were out of the city and in the country.

It had only been a couple minutes ride at most, and Nemo was sure they had covered hundreds of miles. They went through multiple cities, long stretches of flat plains, and up and down mountains. They reached the coast and still did not stop. The horses kept running forward, but did not sink. They ran on top of the ocean, cutting a large wake and spraying water behind them. For much longer than they were on land, they ran across the ocean, until at last they could see land ahead and the horse began to slow.

Nemo looked over the edge of the bed and was delighted to see mermaids keeping pace with them. One turned and waved, Nemo waved back. He looked to the land that they were quickly approaching, and had the sense that this was not any island that existed in the world he knew.

When they reached the shores of the island, Nemo realized that off in the distance he could see the high towers of a golden palace. He realized with excitement that it must be THE Golden Palace. They were close. With the realization, he suddenly felt a touch of nerves and fear. Why did the king request him? What if he was in trouble? Would he be able to leave? Just as these worries began to run through his mind, he felt the bed-chariot lunge and slow down to a stop. Nemo leaned over to see what was wrong. The front wheels had stopped. It seemed his sheet had gotten all wrapped up in the axle.

"Oh, no," said Star Imp, "there's no time for this. We must keep moving. The sun is rising."

"The sun is already up," Nemo said, looking up in the sky. When he looked back at the star imp, he was surprised to see him fading away.

"The real sun," Star Imp said, "and so my time here is done, for now. You can still make it, Nemo. Just take the reins and head straight to the Golden Palace. They are waiting for you. Just don't be distracted, and don't wake up," his last words faded to a whisper, and he was gone.

Nemo urged the night horses to continue, but try as they might, the bed-chariot would not move. He climbed down and tried pull at the stuck sheet, but to no avail. He went behind his bed and tried to push, yelling for the horses to pull, but still nothing. They were not moving with the sheet wrapped around the axle as it was. Just when he was ready to give up, he heard someone calling to him.

"I say, you look like you could use some help there, little Nemo!"

Up on the boardwalk was a clown, with blue striped pants and a red jacket that both seemed a few sizes too big. His face was painted a light green. Nemo didn't think he had ever seen a clown that looked this way before. He wasn't funny. He was short, stocky, and a little tired looking. His makeup was smudged, and his lip protruded from an excessive amount of sunflower seeds. He spit the shells constantly. He wore a derby hat with a card stuck in the band that read "WAKE UP". Nemo didn't feel sure that he should trust the clown, but saw no other option.

"Yes, I'm stuck. Hey, how did you know my name?"

"Everyone here knows your name, kid. Getting you unstuck will be easy. You just need a little help from good old Flip. That's me, by the way, and it's a pleasure to meet you."

The clown approached Nemo's bed, and started inspecting and tugging on the sheet. After a few seconds, he had Nemo grab one end, while he grabbed the other.

Flip offers to help.

"On the count of three, pull."

Nemo did as he said, and when they pulled together, with a pop, the sheet came undone. It really didn't seem like it should have worked the way it did, but when Nemo asked Flip how he did it, Flip just laughed and told him it was a bit of circus magic, whatever that meant.

"Well, thank you. I have to go now. I was on my way to the palace and I'm running out of time," Nemo told Flip.

"Oh, well, you can't just ride up to the palace. The guards would stop you for sure. Turn you around, no doubt. Have you arrested even, put you in the dungeons I would guess. You'd be stuck there forever, never see your parents again, I'm sure of it."

"But... but they're expecting me. I was invited by the king," Nemo explained, a little worried now.

"No, no, no. That can't be right.

Message got mixed up for sure. Wake up, Nemo, nobody just shows up to Slumberland and sees the king. No, you were invited to Slumberland with a chance to meet the king, not invited to the palace by him. Doesn't that sound right?"

The clown talked fast and Nemo began to feel confused. He was sure he remembered what Oomp had told him, but he didn't want to risk being thrown into a dungeon. He wasn't sure what to do. He told Flip as much.

"Wake up Nemo, help is right in front of you. I know a way to get to the palace. There is a grand event at the Slumberland Grand Circus. A chariot race and you just happen to have a chariot and two of the best night horses I've ever seen. You're sure to win. Guess what the prize for the winner is? A day in the palace and lunch with the king! I can get you in, no problem. Just let me hop on board and I'll take you there."

Nemo scratched his chin as he thought. A chariot race sure did sound like a fun adventure. Also, he had the night horses, which could beat anything in a race, as long as he didn't go too fast and lose control like last time. Finally, he nodded and shook Flip's hand. Flip jumped onto the bed-chariot. He took the reins, and called out, "Somnus, Hypnos, to the Grand Circus," and with a flick of his wrist they were off.

****

When they reached the stadium, Flip jumped off. He had stopped them in front of a large iron gate. On the other side of the gate was a broad dirt path that went down under the stadium. Flip explained to Nemo that it was the entrance for the charioteers, and that it came back up in the middle of the stadium. The gate was closed and guarded by two soldiers in ancient roman style armor. Flip left Nemo to go talk to the guards, and after a few minutes came back and wished Nemo luck as the gates opened.

"Flip, I'm a little scared. I've never raced in a chariot before."

"Don't worry kid, you'll be a natural. Nothing can go wrong," he said as he smacked the horse's flanks and they started to walk through the gates. When they were on the other side, Flip closed the gates and the guards locked them once more. "No turning back now, and like I said kid, nothing can go wrong. When you crash, you'll just wake up," and Flip walked away laughing.

"Crash? Wake up? But I'm supposed to go to the palace. Flip? FLIP!" as Nemo yelled, the horses

Nemo dreams of falling after losing control of Somnus.

continued to descend the ramp it grew dark and quiet, taking Nemo out of sight and out of hearing range of Flip.

Nemo felt them begin to ascend, and could hear the sound of rolling thunder. He saw the light on the path ahead, and still the sound of thunder grew louder and louder. When he was nearly to the top of the path, he realized it was not thunder, but the cheering and clapping of tens of thousands of fans. He came up into the center of the stadium. Other chariot racers were already there, three of them, lined up at the starting line. Each chariot was different, as were the charioteers and what was pulling them. The first's driver looked to be a walrus, very large, very fat. He wore a silver helmet with a blue brush plume on its top. He barely fit into his chariot, with the sides of his belly bulging out of the side. His chariot was pulled by two very large turtles. The second charioteer was a large silverback guerilla with golden armor, and a golden helmet with a red brush plume. His chariot was pulled by two bull elephants with large tusks and armor of their own. The third charioteer Nemo had met before. It was the lemur he had raced on his first attempt to enter Slumberland, and his chariot was pulled by a kangaroos and a cat, surely the same ones who had carried him and the frog.

As Nemo emerged from the tunnel with his bed-chariot and two night horses, the crowd cheered even louder. They began to chant his name "NEMO! NEMO! NEMO!" and he wondered how it was that everyone knew his name. Somnus and Hypnos seemed to know exactly what to do,

The pair of elephants powers a racing chariot.

and took the open spot at the starting line. Nemo found himself between the walrus and guerilla. The walrus looked down at Nemo and gave a nod. Nemo looked up to the guerilla, and was greeted with a growl and flashing of teeth. Nemo swallowed hard and set his eyes forward. He was surprised to see Flip on a platform above the crowd. Horns blew and the crowd went silent.

Flip used a long speaking trumpet to address the crowd, "Ladies and gentlemen, man and beast, real and imaginary, welcome to the Grand Circus!" the crowd erupted with applause and Flip waited for them to quiet before continuing, "The grand prize for today's victor is a trip to the Golden Palace and an audience with the king himself. Without further ado, on the trumpets sound let us begin!"

The crowd roared once more, but

this time did not stop. Nemo felt excited, nervous, and scared all at the same time as he waited for the trumpets. They sounded, and the chariots took off with a rush and the thundering sound of a stampede. Somnus and Hypnos jumped into the lead, only the kangaroo and cat kept close. The elephants fell to a distant third and the turtles seemed to be standing still compared to the others. Nemo let the night horses set their own pace, as it seemed they knew what they were doing. He just held on for the ride. He was beginning to feel confident that they would win, as they came around to finish the first lap. The kangaroo and cat found a bit more speed and pulled up next to the night horses. Nemo looked over to the lemur, who was looking back with a smile.

"Sorry, Nemo," said the lemur.

Nemo started to ask why, but then realized his predicament. The lemur had blocked Nemo in, against the inside track wall, and up ahead, not much past the start line, the walrus had his chariot turned sideways, and the turtles had retreated to their shells. Nemo could either hit the walrus's chariot, or hit the turtle.

"Jump!" he called out to Somnus and Hypnos, and they did, right over the turtle. His bed-chariot launched into the air some as well, and the wheels skipped off of the turtles shell. It threw him a bit sideways, and when he landed the wheels on the left side of the chariot broke off, as well as the shaft and yoke. Somnus and Hypnos broke away, and the chariot slid to a stop sideways.

Nemo sat on his bed in a bit of shock, but still okay. He let out a deep breath, but then heard the unmistakable sound of elephants trumpeting. He looked to his right to see the beasts stampeding towards him, tusks down, closing in fast. He closed his eyes tight, curling up into a ball, and then...

Nothing. Everything was quiet. Nemo opened his eyes and found himself in his bed, in his room. The sun was up. It was Saturday morning and his mother was calling him to come down for breakfast.

****

Morning comes after a night of fantastic dreams.

Wake up!

Also by Nathaniel Matthews

Dakota Black: The Dragon

★★★★★

"A modern reappearance of the great American novel Moby Dick, in a form appealing to today's readers."

-Reedsy.com

★★★★★

"It's a great retelling of the classic tale of Moby Dick, but with a wicked twist that creates such a dark and pulsating tension that readers won't want to stop reading until the last page is read.."

-Jerry Mason (Author of "Baby Eagle")

Made in United States
Troutdale, OR
09/20/2024

23002631R10051